FRED
SAVES THE DAY

Chris

THIS BOOK BELONGS TO
CHRISTOPHER

The Adventures of Fred
Published by Fawcett Columbine

FRED TO THE RESCUE
FRED IN CHARGE
FRED AND THE PET SHOW PANIC
FRED SAVES THE DAY

FRED
SAVES THE DAY

by Leslie McGuire

Illustrated by Dave Henderson

Fawcett Columbine • New York

CONTENTS

CHAPTER ONE

SUMMERTIME BLUES

Well, summer has just officially begun. I could tell that the moment Beth and Arnie and Mike and Katie came into the house. They were stomping their feet. They were yelling and singing a very naughty poem:

No more pencils,
No more books,
No more teacher's dirty looks.
Kick the tables,
Kick the chairs,
Kick the teachers down the stairs.

It was the last day of school. Kids always think this is great. This is not great. When

1

they are home from school, my life starts to go downhill. But does anyone care? No. They do not even notice how hard I work. I don't mean to say the Duffs are bad people. They are wonderful. They are about the best humans you could find on the planet. But they do have some small problems.

Perhaps I should tell you who I am. I am Fred Duff. I am the Duff family dog. I am a Saint Bernard. You know, those dogs who rescue you from disasters like snowstorms and floods. We are supposed to carry a little barrel of brandy under our chins. We are supposed to give the brandy to the people we rescue. Of course, this is a silly thing to do. Brandy is not good for humans. Everyone knows this. Chicken soup would be a lot better. But nobody has ever thought to ask me *my* opinion. They should. I know a lot about humans.

The Duffs live in a town called Big Bluff. There is a reason they call it that. The town has a small harbor and a big bluff—which is really a cliff, if you want my opinion. At the

2

bottom of the bluff, there is a nice muddy marsh. I like to go down there.

I like to wash myself down at the marsh. I roll in seaweed and sand. This is good for the skin. Except for the fact that sometimes you smell like a dead fish, it is very healthy. Try it sometime.

The Duffs' house is on top of the bluff. Sometimes they call it Duff's Bluff. I call it "A Disaster Waiting to Happen." I do not like that bluff. Someone is always getting too close to the edge. They could fall off. I have to rescue them all the time. Especially Mr. Duff. He's always clipping the hedge or mowing the lawn. This is silly. Leave the hedge and the lawn alone, I say. Every time I rescue him, he calls me a fathead. But I don't really mind. Safe is safe, I always say.

Mrs. Duff is not that big a problem. But the two Duff children are constantly in danger. Katie Duff is a teenager. She doesn't even know how to cross a street. I have to rescue her all the time. She says I wreck her hairdo and her outfit. I say, getting hit by a car also wrecks your hairdo and your outfit. Safe is safe.

Arnie Duff is my favorite Duff. He is the youngest Duff. He is a good boy, but careless. He is also short. Arnie is so short that I am taller than Arnie is when Arnie is standing up and I am sitting down.

The big problem with Arnie is that he never looks where he is going. This is not because he can't see. Arnie can see just fine. In fact, he just got glasses last summer.

Before he got his glasses, he couldn't see much at all. Now he can see *everything*. But that only makes things worse. He is always rushing off to get a better look at something completely boring like a crab or an old gum wrapper. I have to rescue him from whatever is between him and the thing he wants to get a better look at.

Actually, the most important thing about Arnie is that I am his dog. In fact, Arnie would not be alive today if it weren't for me. But keeping Arnie alive is very hard work.

Beth and Mike are Arnie's best friends. They spend a lot of time at the Duff house. Therefore, I also have to keep them safe. Beth and Mike are careless, too.

Anyway, where was I? Oh yes. It was the

last day of school, and that meant no rest for Fred. That is why summer is not great. The kids would be around all day, every day. Aaargh.

Summer is also not great for other reasons. For example, it is hot and humid. This feels terrible if you are covered with fur.

I was munching on a copy of *Good Housekeeping.* I always chew paper when I'm feeling upset. And I always read while I chew. Magazines are very interesting. Besides, *Good Housekeeping* is one of my favorites. That is because there are none of those terrible perfume ads in that magazine. Believe me, perfume ads taste disgusting. Don't ever eat one.

I was trying to read an article called "Special Summer Tips for Your Pet." It was about ways to take care of your pet during the hot weather. There were a lot of dumb ideas which I hope the Duffs never find out about.

For example, they suggested extra baths. I hate baths.

They also said it was a good idea to put flea powder on your pet. Summer is flea season. But who cares? Flea powder smells nasty and makes me sneeze. It was a bad idea.

They also said it was a good idea to keep your pet indoors, where it is cool. Now, *that* was the dumbest idea they had yet. I quickly ate the page. I did not want the Duffs to get any more silly ideas.

In addition, Fudge was pestering me. As usual. Did I mention Fudge? I guess not. That is because I wish I didn't have to think about Fudge—ever again. Fudge is a cat.

Fudge calls me "Mom." This is very annoying. He has also forced me to give him reading lessons. I know this is a mistake. There are no good cats. But if there were such a thing as a good cat, it would be a dumb cat. And there is only one thing worse than a dumb cat. That is a smart cat.

I only agreed to teach Fudge to read because I thought he would never be able to learn. Unfortunately, Fudge turned out to be good at reading. Now that silly cat wants to read all the time. Even worse, he wants to read out loud! It breaks my concentration.

Anyway, while I was reading my article, I overheard something awful.

The Duffs were planning a picnic at the park for tomorrow! My heart sank.

The park can be a very dangerous place!

CHAPTER TWO

HOUDINI DOES IT AGAIN

I hoped the kids were wrong about the picnic. They were not. When I woke up on Saturday morning, the kitchen was filled with stuff. There were paper plates, paper cups, and bags of chips. There were picnic baskets, hampers, and coolers. There were bags of stuff and bowls of stuff.

And it was very early—only eight o'clock. That meant they were going to spend a whole day at the park! This trip would be filled with disaster. The Duffs were planning to spend eight or ten hours at the park. That meant at least forty disasters—all in one day. I was tired just thinking about it.

The next thing I knew, Beth and Mike

9

came over. That meant two extra people to rescue. I watched the Duffs pack tons of stuff in the car. I decided I'd better pack some stuff of my own. I needed a few things in case of difficult rescues.

I went into the garage and found my special rope. That is very good for things like falling off cliffs, or falling down holes. I quickly stuffed the rope under the front seat of the car. It was a bit dirty. I was afraid if someone found it, they would toss it out of the car. I was just going to get some of my other rescue equipment when I heard Mrs. Duff shout.

"Are we ready, gang?"

I knew what that meant. I jumped into the front seat.

"Oh, no you don't," said Katie, opening the car door. "Out, Fred! You're not coming!"

I didn't move. I knew Arnie or Mrs. Duff would not leave me behind.

"Out you go, Fred," said Mr. Duff.

Forget it, I thought. I am here to stay.

But I was wrong. When Mrs. Duff and the rest of the kids came out, they *all* told me to get out.

"Sorry, boy," said Arnie. "But you can't come this time."

Were they crazy? This was the one time they really needed me to come. Did they have any idea how dangerous it was at the park? I guess not.

I was insulted. I was upset. But that did not stop me.

"Are you going to lock him in the house?" asked Katie.

"He always gets out of the house," said Mrs. Duff.

"Well, he always gets out of the garage, too," said Katie.

"Not anymore," said Mr. Duff. "I fixed that back window."

What? Suddenly I didn't feel quite as sure. But I was still not too worried. After all, I thought, the Great Houdini of Dogs is never stopped by small problems. Working latches and locks was easy. After all, I managed to break out of Dog Jail, didn't I? But that is another story. I was sure this breakout would be a lot easier than that one.

I let the Duffs put me in the garage. I let them lock the door. I heard them all get in the car and drive off. I looked up at the window. Fudge was sitting outside on the sill. He was looking in at me. It looked like he was laughing. But I did not care. I was too busy working on a plan.

I needed someplace comfortable to sit. I jumped into Mr. Duff's car. The Duffs have two cars. The old one is Mr. Duff's. He uses it to go to work. The new one is for Mrs. Duff. It is a station wagon. The whole family is very excited by Mrs. Duff's new car. They call it the Duff-Mobile. I don't like it that much. As far as I'm concerned, it smells too new. I like a car that smells a bit more lived-in. I will have to work on the new car.

I settled down on the front seat of the old car. Then I happened to notice the little square box on the dashboard. That is when I had my plan!

You see, when the Duffs got the new station wagon, they also decided to fix up the garage.

I have to say something here about garages. A garage is really a house for a car. This is silly.

Anyway, where was I? Oh yes. My plan.

They fixed up the garage. That included getting an automatic garage door opener. That was what the little square thing was. There were two garage door openers. One was in the station wagon with the Duffs. One was in the old car with me.

I stood up and shoved the garage door opener off the dashboard. I knocked it onto the front seat. I pushed the little button with my nose.

Voilà! The garage door opened. I, Fred, the Great Houdini of Dogs, the Savior of the Duffs, and the Protector of the Careless, had done it again. I was on my way to the park!

CHAPTER THREE

FOUR SNAKES AND NO CHARCOAL

I knew exactly where the Duffs were headed. They were going to the state park on Highway 31. It was not far away. But it is even closer the way I go.

For one thing, a dog does not do well running along Highway 31. Nobody does. Lots of cars don't do that well, either. You read about car crashes all the time in the paper.

I ran down to Main Street. I took a quick left on Hill Street. I shot into the woods. I went through a few open fields. I took the straightest route to the state park. I cut at least half an hour off the trip by car. I ran very fast. I was hoping I got to the Duffs before they did anything dangerous.

You probably think they wouldn't have enough time to get in trouble. That is where you are wrong. The Duffs can get in trouble in only one minute—that is, if I'm not around.

I flew out of the woods. I was on the edge of the big parking lot. I found the Duffs' station wagon. Now all I had to do was find the Duffs. This was not hard. There is an area that has picnic tables. It is best to get your picnic table early. Otherwise, millions of people show up. Well, maybe not millions, but at least hundreds. There are only about twenty-five picnic tables. This causes problems. I have seen people fight over a picnic table. Now, isn't that a dumb thing to fight over, I ask you?

I found the Duffs. And just in time. Mr. Duff was trying to build a fire. Fortunately, Mrs. Duff had forgotten to bring the bag of charcoal. Mrs. Duff forgets things a lot. This is one of the good things about Mrs. Duff. She forgets to put food away. Naturally, I have to keep an eye on her.

After all, food that gets left out will go bad. If a person eats it, he will get sick. I protect my family at all times from all things. Therefore, I eat whatever Mrs. Duff forgets to put away. I do this to keep the family from getting sick. It is for their own good, of course. I am a very noble dog. They don't always look at it that way, but safe is safe.

"Hey, Ma!" yelled Arnie. "It's Fred!"

Katie looked grouchy. Mr. Duff looked as if smoke were about to come out of his ears.

"Well," Mr. Duff said in a crabby voice. "Fred will just have to stay. I'm not going to drive him all the way back home again."

I knew they would see it my way.

I suppose I should tell you about Mr. Duff. He is big and round and bald. He wears glasses like Arnie's. He likes to pretend that he is grouchy. But he really is a very kind man. I enjoy his company. I know that he enjoys my company, too. He just doesn't always like to admit it.

Well, I thought, everything would be fine without charcoal. After all, who needs cooked food? But I did not count on Arnie. He is a Boy Scout. Boy Scouts learn all sorts of useless things, like building fires, pitching tents, making baskets, and cooking.

"We don't need charcoal," Arnie piped up. "We'll just go collect some wood!"

As soon as Arnie said that, the kids galloped off into the woods. It was a very good thing I had arrived when I did. I followed right behind them. The woods could be very dangerous.

We went down a little path. The path was lined with very nice ferns. There were old logs, and pale gray mushrooms. I was sure the mushrooms were poisonous. But Beth wasn't looking for sticks. She started poking around in the logs.

Suddenly I heard this little squeak from Beth.

"Ooooh, look!" she said. "Snakes!"

Snakes? I do not like snakes. I don't trust anything that doesn't have feet.

I suppose I should explain about Beth. Beth is not a normal little girl. She loves animals. This is good. But she is always rescuing animals that don't need any rescuing. She rescues spiders and frogs and beetles. Spiders and frogs and beetles do not need rescuing. They are better off right where they are.

Beth says that we are alike. But we are not. She rescues animals that don't need rescuing. I only rescue things that *do* need rescuing. But she does not look at it that way.

Beth lives in a big house with lots and lots of pets. Her father is a scientist. He collects things like spiders and snakes and frogs. Beth thinks they are sweet. I think they are boring. But at least Beth's heart is in the right place. She just gets confused sometimes. This was one of those times. She had uncovered a nest of baby snakes.

"Oh, goody!" Beth squealed. "I'll take them home!"

I rushed over. Beth was about to rescue those baby snakes. I didn't know who needed rescuing more—Beth or the baby snakes. After all, some snakes bite. But those snakes looked pretty harmless. I saved the

baby snakes by dragging Beth away by the seat of her pants.

"Good boy!" yelled Arnie. He thought I was saving Beth.

When we got back to the picnic table, Arnie told Mr. and Mrs. Duff what a great job I had done.

"He saved Beth!" said Arnie. "Those snakes could have been poisonous. Fred dragged her away before she could get bitten."

I let everyone pet me and hug me. I was not about to tell them those baby snakes were just harmless garter snakes. I happen to know a poisonous snake when I see one. After all, I read *Natural History* magazine.

I just felt that I have enough responsibility with all the Duffs to watch, plus Fudge. I didn't want to worry about five homeless baby snakes on top of it all.

CHAPTER FOUR

FORGET ABOUT FIRE!

The kids made five or six more trips to collect sticks and twigs. I, of course, followed them. There were no more problems. At least not on the twig-collecting trips. The real problems came later.

When we got back with the last load of sticks, Arnie made a special pile in the fire pit. He learned this trick in Boy Scouts. They should be careful what they teach children.

He placed a whole bunch of sticks in a pyramid shape. It looked just like an Indian teepee. Well, while Arnie was doing this, Mrs. Duff was poking around in all the boxes, baskets, hampers, and bags. She was muttering.

Mr. Duff was back at the car. He was getting the last few things we needed for the picnic.

"Okay, Ma," said Arnie as he put the last stick in place. "It's ready! Let's light the fire!"

But Mrs. Duff kept right on poking around.

"I know I put those matches someplace in here," she said as she poked.

Well, soon everyone was looking for the matches. Mr. Duff looked through everything that Mrs. Duff had just looked through. Mr. Duff does not believe that Mrs. Duff forgets things. He believes she just forgets where she *puts* things. I know better. That is because usually the things she forgets end up in my stomach. I am the only one who knows where the things are. But I don't tell.

This time, however, I did not know where the matches were. I do not eat matches.

But I did not think this was a problem. What is the point of fire? Mr. and Mrs. Duff were getting crankier and crankier by the

24

minute. But the kids did not seem to mind either. After all, there was still a lot of food to eat.

Arnie pointed out that you don't have to cook potato salad, or chips. Beth said cold lemonade is better than hot lemonade. Even Katie laughed at that one. Then Katie said she would eat the hot dog buns cold. And Mike said he never did like charcoal-broiled chocolate chip cookies anyway. All the kids were giggling.

I didn't much mind either. After all, what did we need a fire for? No fire meant that all the hot dogs were left for me, right? I have no problem with eating raw hot dogs. Besides, raw hot dogs aren't really raw anyway. They are already sort of cooked. They are smoked. That is what gives them such a nice flavor. Although now I do remember reading an article in *Prevention* magazine about hot dog flavor. It said the smoke flavor came from chemicals.

Well, all the more reason for me, Fred, the

Protector of the Duffs, to eat up all the hot dogs. Right?

That reminded me of another article I saw. This one was in *Woman's Day.* By the way, that is another very good magazine. Tasty, I mean. They don't have perfume ads in that one, either. Perfume ads should be banned. After all, I may not be the only reader who likes to chew on a magazine now and then. But does anyone think about us magazine chewers and our right to a tasty magazine? Nope.

Anyway, this article was about how charcoal is bad for people. It said all that black stuff on the outside of your food may taste good, but it makes you sick.

I decided it was a good thing Mrs. Duff forgot the matches. The entire family would be better off without fire. Besides, I do not see why humans won't eat raw meat. I eat raw meat. I don't mind. Humans are just too picky.

Furthermore, fires are dangerous. The Duffs could accidentally start a forest fire, right? Isn't Smokey Bear always telling people to be careful with fire? Well, here is the most careful thing you can do with fire: Do not have one at all.

I decided this picnic was not going to be so dangerous after all. I mean, if there was no fire, what could possibly go wrong?

Guess.

CHAPTER FIVE

HUNG BY MY OWN RESCUE ROPE

I thought the day would go smoothly. That is when things started to go wrong. First, the kids all ran to the lake. I, of course, followed them. They were not wearing bathing suits. That was good. No one goes swimming without a bathing suit in the Duff family. However, they still had to be watched. Accidents happen—especially when you get too near large bodies of water.

Katie sat on a big rock. She looked at her reflection in the lake. She started fussing with her hair. Katie will use anything for a mirror. When she looks in a window, she is not looking to see what's inside. She is looking at herself. That girl is more interested in her hairdo than anyone I have ever seen.

Then Mike got out his camera. He was sneaking up on frogs and grasshoppers. He wanted to get close-ups. Mike is like a Saint Bernard, too. But he is different from Beth and me. He doesn't rescue anyone. He just carries a camera hanging around his neck all the time. That's instead of a barrel of brandy.

The frogs and grasshoppers he was sneaking up on didn't seem to want to get their pictures taken. But maybe they were afraid of Beth. She was sneaking up on them, too. Maybe they could tell she was about to rescue them, and take them home, and keep them in a cage forever. She had that "I'm about to save your life" look in her eye. Those animals were not as dumb as they looked.

Anyway, Arnie found a rowboat. It even had oars in it. Arnie and the kids wanted to get right in. This, of course, was out of the question. Each time one of them tried to get in the boat, I dragged them out. They yelled and carried on. But I paid no attention. Safe is safe.

"Aw, c'mon!" howled Arnie.

"Let go of me!" screeched Beth.

"We just want to sit in it for a minute," whined Mike.

I did not care what they said. They were not getting in that boat.

Finally Arnie raced off to tell Mr. and Mrs. Duff that they wanted to go out in the boat. I figured Mr. and Mrs. Duff would tell them they weren't allowed. But again, I was wrong. Mr. and Mrs. Duff thought it was a great idea. They even decided to come along for the ride!

Personally, I think that going out in a row-boat is a crazy idea. All that deep water. All those open sides to fall over. Crazy. Just crazy.

To make matters worse, they were *all* planning to get in the boat. There would be four kids and two adults in that little bitty boat!

Even someone who is not a safety nut can see how dumb that is!

Well, I barked. I got between them and the boat. I pulled everyone away. I ran around in circles. I knocked a few of them down. But it did no good.

Mr. Duff got very angry. He finally went stomping off to the car. I thought the whole plan to go for a ride in the boat was over. I was wrong. Mr. Duff came back with a rope.

My rope!

He took the rope I was planning to rescue them with. He tied me to a tree!

Well, I have never been so upset in my entire life. There I was, stuck on the land. I was tied to a tree. All I wanted to do was keep those silly people safe. But they tied me with my own rescue rope.

I had to sit there and watch them take that silly rowboat out into the middle of the lake.

Let me describe to you what the rowboat looked like with all those people in it.

Usually a boat sticks up out of the water

at least a foot or two. That rowboat, with big Mr. Duff, big Mrs. Duff, medium-sized Katie, medium-sized Mike, small Beth, and tiny Arnie, was barely visible. Maybe an inch of wood stuck up all the way around. It looked like they were sitting in a shallow hole in the water. If one of them sneezed, the boat would probably sink.

The Duffs were doomed.

CHAPTER SIX

ANOTHER GENIUS RESCUE

If it hadn't been so dangerous, I would have thought it was funny.

The whole family was out on the lake. Mr. Duff was rowing. The boat was almost sinking. They were zigging this way. They were zagging that way. It looked ridiculous.

The boat was full. It was heavy. Mr. Duff was pulling way too hard on the oars. One of the oars popped out of the oarlock. Naturally, Mr. Duff let go of the oar. Of course, it fell into the water and floated away.

While the Duffs were in the boat, I was working on the rope. I had one eye on the Duffs and one eye on the rope. At first, I tried to untie the knot. This is usually a simple process. Just hook one of your eyeteeth through one of the loops. Pull, and the rope unties. This works very well with Mr. Duff's special slipknot. Mr. Duff thinks it is the best knot in the world. I think it is the worst knot in the world. But I would be the last one to tell him that.

Anyway, I gave up trying to untie the rope. My rescue rope was too thick. I had to chew my way through it as fast as I could.

"Oh dear," yipped Mrs. Duff as the oar floated away. She clasped her hand over her mouth. "Now what will we do?"

"Don't worry," said Mr. Duff in his deep voice. He always uses his deep voice when he wants everyone to know that he has everything under control. Usually, when I hear his deep voice, I know that he has nothing under control. I chewed harder.

"But how are you going to row, Dad?" asked Arnie.

"I will paddle with one oar," said Mr. Duff. "No problem."

So then Mr. Duff started to paddle. He

35

dipped the oar in the water on one side of the boat. Then he quickly passed it over everyone's heads and dipped it in the water on the other side of the boat. The oar dripped water. Arnie was getting wet. But worse, Katie was getting wet.

In the middle of one of the passes, Arnie suddenly spotted something in the water.

"Hey, look!" he said. He jumped and leaned over the edge to get a better look. "It's a sunny in a plastic bag!"

In case you don't know what a sunny is, it's a smallish fish that lives in freshwater lakes. What it was doing in a plastic bag, I do not know. The fish was not important. The important part of this is what happened when Arnie stood up. He banged into the oar, and it flew out of Mr. Duff's hands. It fell into the water. It floated away.

Now the Duff family was stranded in the middle of the lake. They did not have any oars! Arnie didn't even notice.

By this time, Beth was hanging over the

37

side of the boat, too. She stuck her hand in the water. She picked something up.

"Look!" she said. "I caught the sunny! It must have swum into this plastic sandwich bag by accident."

All the garbage humans throw into lakes and rivers is hurting the fish.

That poor sunny could only swim forward. He swam into the plastic bag because he couldn't see it under water. Then he couldn't get out. For once, Beth had rescued an animal that really *did* need to be rescued. I was very proud of her. Besides, fish are no problem. They stay in their fish tanks. A fish would not be my responsibility. I decided to let her keep the fish.

But I couldn't worry about the fish just yet. I had to worry about the Duffs. They were still stranded in the boat.

"Daaaddddyyyyy!" cried Katie. "Now what did you do!"

"Don't worry," said Mike, grinning. "You can always swim to shore."

"What?" squeaked Katie. "What about my hair?"

"Hair is not the problem," said Beth, looking gloomy. "What about my new pet fish? I have to get him home quick."

"Forget about the fish," said Mrs. Duff. "How are we going to get back? We aren't wearing bathing suits."

"Forget about bathing suits," said Arnie. "Even if we were wearing them, the water is freeeeezing!"

"Forget about the freezing water," said Mike. "I can't get my camera wet!"

"Don't worry," said Mr. Duff. "We'll be back on the shore in no time."

Finally I got the rope chewed through. It was a very thick rope. That is why I brought it. You need a strong rope for rescues. You need a weak rope to get tied up with. If I had known what the rope would be used for, I would have brought a weak one. But things do not always work out the way I plan them.

"How are we going to get to shore?" asked Katie.

"The current will take us," said Arnie.

"What current?" said Beth.

Mr. Duff did not say anything at all.

Anyway, I finally raced down to the lake and jumped in. I had to rescue my poor hopeless family. I swam right out to the row-boat. I hoped the Duffs could manage to stay in the boat until I got there.

CHAPTER SEVEN

ANOTHER UNGRATEFUL DUFF

I swam out to the boat, barking as I went. I was telling them all to sit down. I was telling them to stay calm. I was telling them not to worry. Of course, they did not listen. Arnie stood up. Mrs. Duff was wringing her hands. Katie was moaning. Mr. Duff was looking grouchy.

Sometimes I think Mr. Duff looks grouchy because things are not going the way he planned them. I understand this. In some ways, Mr. Duff and I are a lot alike. The only difference is that I have more hair, and he has less sense.

Well, I got to the boat. The cold water felt pretty nice. As I said earlier, hot weather is not great when you are covered with fur. I do not always get a chance to go swimming. I reminded myself to do this more often.

I swam around the boat a few times. I barked. Finally Mr. Duff got my message. He untied the anchor. He threw the anchor rope out of the front of the rowboat. It hit the water with a smack. I grabbed it in my teeth.

Now came the hard part. Towing a boat is not hard. But towing a boat full of humans is very hard. But hard does not mean impossible. I, Fred, the Great Houdini of Dogs and the Savior of the Duffs, can do anything. It does not matter how hard it is.

But for a minute, I thought my teeth would fall out. They did not. I figured that at least I would get a good lunch as a reward. The one thing that kept me going was the thought of all those nice, raw hot dogs waiting for me on the picnic table. It made me swim harder.

Soon I had the boat safely near the shore. Of course, everyone stood up at once. The boat started to rock. I started to bark. So did Mr. Duff. I don't mean that Mr. Duff actually barked. It just sounded like a bark. Everyone sat down.

"One at a time," said Mr. Duff. "Me first."

And with that, Mr. Duff stepped out of the boat. He pulled it closer to the shore. One by one, the family got out of the boat.

Then Katie got up and started to point. Katie was in the back, so I knew she needed some help. As she stepped over the edge, I got right next to her. I wanted her to put her hand on my back. This would keep her from falling. Instead, Katie put her foot on my back. She wasn't even looking. She was still squeaking and pointing. I wish Katie would learn to pay attention, but I guess that will take a few more years.

Anyway, when she put her foot on my back, she slipped. She fell out of the boat. She landed in the water.

Maybe I should describe what the edge of the lake was like. This was not a sandybottom lake. The bottom was muddy. There were lots of reeds. There were all these slimy underwater plants. There were a few snails in there too.

I don't suppose I have to tell you that Katie got pretty wet. In fact, she got one half of herself *all* wet.

Then she started to yell at *me!*

"Now look what you made me do!" she howled. She tried to stand up. But she slipped in the mud again. That's when the other half of her got all wet. Then she started to cry.

Now, one of my big problems is that I have never been able to resist a crying human. I raced up to her as she scrambled onto shore. I gave her a big kiss.

"Don't kiss me!" she yelled. "You are all muddy!"

What difference did a little more mud make? After all, she was muddier and wetter than I was, right? I will never understand teenagers. My feelings were hurt.

Of course, as soon as Katie fell in the

water, Mike had his camera out. He took some pretty good pictures. I hoped he got one or two of me towing the boat as well. That was something the newspaper could *really* use.

I always bring a few of my rescue photos down to the local newspaper office. So far they haven't done a front-page story on me. But I think they are waiting until they have at least fifty pictures. I bet they are planning to write an entire *issue* about me, Fred. I can just see the headline now: FRED SAVES THE DAY—EVERY DAY! Or maybe it will say: FRED GETS A PURPLE HEART! Or even: FRED, THE BEST RESCUE DOG THE WORLD HAS EVER KNOWN!

But let me get back to the story. Anyway, I felt so bad about Katie crying, I raced into the boat. Mr. Duff's jacket was on one of the seats. I grabbed it and carried it to Katie. She was cold. Her shorts and her T-shirt were all wet. I didn't want her to get sick. Unfortunately, the sleeve of Mr. Duff's jacket caught on the end of a stump. The sleeve tore off.

Mr. Duff started to yell. I could not understand his problem. Did he want his daughter to catch a cold? True, it was sad that the sleeve came off his jacket. But the rest of the jacket was warm and dry. It was certainly better than wearing wet shorts and a wet T-shirt, right?

But that was not the reason Mr. Duff was yelling. Now he was pointing at the picnic table, too.

I decided I had better take a look. This is what I saw.

A very big mess.

CHAPTER EIGHT

MUGGED BY SQUIRRELS

We had been robbed by squirrels!

I knew something looked odd when Katie first pointed. But that was right before she stepped on my back. I wasn't thinking about food right then. I was still thinking about rescuing. Rescuing takes up my whole brain when I'm in the middle of it.

Anyway, everyone ran over to the picnic table.

There was a mess, all right. The squirrels had stolen everything. Whatever food they did not steal had little squirrel footprints in it.

The squirrels ran off with the hot dog buns. They ate all the chocolate chip cookies and the marshmallows. Katie, Arnie, and Beth went crazy when they saw the empty boxes.

"Now we have nothing at *all* to eat," howled Arnie.

"I was really looking forward to eating those cookies," said Mike sadly.

"It's all *your* fault," said Katie, staring at me.

My fault? How was it my fault? I ask you.

"Fred should have stayed here and guarded the food. Instead, he was knocking me into the lake," yelled Katie. "Now we have no food to eat!"

"That's not true," said Mrs. Duff. "It isn't Fred's fault. Fred saved us."

"That's right," said Arnie. He gave me a hug even though I was wet and muddy. Arnie is really the best boy on the planet. "If it wasn't for Fred, we'd all still be out in the middle of the lake."

"The squirrels have been stamping in the potato salad," said Mr. Duff. "I refuse to eat potato salad with squirrel footprints in it."

He was awfully fussy. I would not have minded that. But I share food with squirrels a lot. The dumpster down by the supermarket has some pretty good snacks from time to time. But the snacks usually have a few footprints in them. Sometimes it pays to learn to be less fussy about what you eat.

I would have eaten the potato salad, but I don't like potato salad. Too much vinegar. It makes my ears curl up when I eat it. Besides, the Duffs could always scrape off the footprints. I still had the hot dogs, right?

Wrong.

The squirrels had run off with both packages of hot dogs, too! Now I was mad. There should really be a law against squirrels in the park.

Those squirrels had scattered all the chips on the grass and knocked over the lemonade as well. There was nothing left for the Duffs—or me.

Katie was wet and mad. The rest of them were dry and hungry. I was wet and hungry.

And tired. There was absolutely nothing left to do but start cleaning the mess.

I saw a squirrel or two hanging around the table. I chased after them, barking and snarling. But it was too late.

Then Mr. Duff had a good idea.

"Let's tidy up," he said. "Then we'll go over to that little food stand on the other side of the lake."

"Good thinking, Dad," said Arnie.

"It's a long walk," said Katie.

"It's better than starving," said Mike.

"I'll bring my bug jar," said Beth, looking very cheered up. "Maybe I'll find some interesting spiders on the way."

I decided it was a good plan, too. The garbage cans near food stands are always filled with good snacks. Besides, I could see that I wasn't going to get lunch any other way.

Mr. and Mrs. Duff and Arnie and Katie and Mike and Beth started to clean up. With all of them working together, it didn't take too long. I helped, naturally. I gave instructions.

We collected the hamper, the picnic baskets, and the cooler. We picked up the scattered potato chips. We put the top back on the bowl of potato salad. We folded all the paper bags so they wouldn't blow into the lake. We shook out the tablecloth, and put it back on the table. We found the paper plates that didn't have footprints on them. We collected the paper cups.

"Hey, look!" shouted Beth from under a bush.

I didn't bother to check on what she had found. I figured it was some poor bug she was about to rescue. So did everyone else.

Then Beth came running over. She had found a bag of chips under the bush. It was full.

Everyone wanted one. Katie stuck her hand in the bag, and then she screamed.

"Ants!"

Katie threw the bag to the ground.

I would have eaten them. But even I, Fred, do not eat ants. They are bitter. Besides, I had recently been trying to cut the amount of salt in my snacks. I read an article in *Prevention* magazine about how salt raises blood pressure. I think my blood pressure is high enough. I don't need salty potato chips. I have enough stress from watching out for the Duffs.

I figured a nice quiet walk would calm me down. We were halfway around the lake, heading to the food stand. That's when a big, fat raindrop hit me on the nose.

CHAPTER NINE

SOAKED AND ALMOST SHOCKED

You would think that before planning an all-day, outdoor picnic, someone would have checked the weather report.

I looked up. The sky was gray. Big, lumpy-looking clouds were zipping around up there. It did not look promising.

I have found that there is never one big, fat raindrop. A big, fat raindrop is usually followed by about five thousand more big, fat raindrops. As usual, I was right.

"Oh dear," said Mrs. Duff. "Does this mean it's going to rain?"

The whole family stopped and looked up. A few more fat raindrops fell.

"It's probably just a passing cloud," said Mr. Duff. "Let's keep going."

It was not a passing cloud. It was the most amazing rainstorm I have ever seen.

First a few more raindrops fell. Then a small gust of wind came up. Then there was a flash of light and a loud crack of thunder. Lightning!

Now, you don't have to read too many newspaper articles to know how dangerous lightning is. It is especially dangerous around lakes. This big bolt of jagged light came out of the sky. Katie screamed. Beth dropped her bug jar. Mike tried to stuff his camera into his shirt. Arnie, of course, went running off.

Of course, Arnie went running off because he wanted a better look at the lightning. This is very wrong. I ran right after him. I grabbed him by the sleeve. I dragged him back to the family.

Then water started to pour out of the sky. The water wasn't like rain at all. It was more

like being under Niagara Falls. There was so much water.

Of course, the first thing Katie did was run under a tree. The last place anyone should run during a lightning storm is under a tree. I have read many, many articles about this. In case you don't know why, I will tell you.

Lightning likes to strike the tallest thing around. Usually, the tallest thing around is a building or a tree. That is why tall buildings have these little sticks on the top made of metal. The sticks have a wire running all the way down the building into the ground. They are called lightning rods. The lightning rod attracts the lightning. It sends all the electricity down into the ground, where it can't hurt anything.

If you don't have a lightning rod, all that electricity goes into whatever it hits. Usually it burns that thing to a crisp. This is not a good thing to have happen to you. If you are standing under a tree that gets hit by lightning, you will also be burned to a crisp. For that reason, the best place to be is in a car.

I grabbed Katie and dragged her away from the tree. Then I started barking at the rest of the family. It was time for another rescue.

I ran around them to get them in a clump. Then I started barking at their heels. They all started to run to get away from me. I chased them back around the lake. I chased them to the picnic table.

"Quick!" said Mrs. Duff. "Get all the things collected."

"Get in the car!" yelled Mr. Duff. Mr. Duff was tripping over things. That is because his glasses had water pouring down them. So did Arnie's glasses. They should invent windshield wipers for glasses. Those two can't see without their glasses. What are they supposed to do when they can't see *with* their glasses?

I decided I would work on that invention tomorrow. Now I had to make sure they all got safely to the car.

It only took about three seconds to grab all the stuff. Then they all made a mad dash for the parking lot. Of course, this was a problem. The Duffs were not the only people at the park. There were hundreds of families. They were all jumping into their cars. They were all driving around the parking lot. The rain was making it hard for anyone to see where they were going. It was crazy.

The Duffs were on the sidewalk, where they belonged. The cars were on the streets, where they belonged. But this did not matter. The cars were not being driven by normal people. They were being driven by cranky, wet, and careless people.

I kept the Duffs near the inside edge of the sidewalk. I had to do this the only way I have ever found to work. I had to shove them into the bushes now and then.

I kept getting yelled at.

"FRED!" yelled Arnie. "Don't push me!"

"Cut that out, you fathead!" yelled Mr. Duff.

"Let go of my shorts!" yelled Beth.

"Ma, he's getting mud all over me!" yelled Katie.

This last remark was silly. Katie already had mud all over her.

I finally got them safely to the car. They threw all the picnic stuff into the back. Then everyone got inside and slammed the doors.

"Oh dear," Mrs. Duff finally said, after looking around. "Just look at my brand-new car!"

She did not look happy. I could see why. The inside of the car looked like a sandbox after a mud fight. But I noticed that it smelled a lot better. The new car smell was almost all gone.

"We should call it the mud-mobile instead of the Duff-Mobile!" said Arnie. He thought that was pretty funny. I thought it was pretty funny, too.

Nobody else thought it was funny at all.

CHAPTER TEN

HOME IS SAFE—FOR SOME

It was still pouring rain when we got home. Mr. Duff drove the station wagon right into the garage.

"Hey, how come the garage door is open?" he mumbled as he stopped the car. "I could have sworn I left it shut. . . ."

Then he gave me a very suspicious look. I gave him back a very innocent look. He shook his head.

"I better check that garage door opener," he muttered. "Maybe water got into the wires. Maybe something shorted out."

I smiled. That would probably keep him busy and out of trouble for an hour or so. And it wouldn't change anything. I would still be able to get at the garage door opener if necessary. That is one of the great things about summer. The car windows are always rolled down.

But I reminded myself to figure out a way to get into the car just in case the windows were rolled up. After all, winter would soon be here. The only way to make sure you can escape from anything is to plan ahead! They don't call me the Great Houdini of Dogs by accident, you know.

Anyway, everyone looked like a mud ball by the time we got into the kitchen. They tracked mud in the house. They left puddles of dirty water all over everything. Mrs. Duff made everyone strip down to their underwear in the kitchen. Then she got them all towels and clean clothes. Katie refused, of course. But she agreed to take off her sneakers before she went upstairs.

Soon, all the Duffs were dry. Arnie came down with Katie's blow dryer. He was planning to dry me, too. Fortunately, Katie made him give it back before he had a chance to do too much damage. I hate the blow dryer. It always makes me feel like a complete fuzz ball.

Anyway, then Mrs. Duff got out a whole bunch of very tasty leftovers. She spread them all out on the back porch table. The rain couldn't get through the screens. It was a very nice picnic. Actually, I think this is the best kind of picnic to have. After all, it is outside. It is certainly the safest place I can think of for the Duffs. Unfortunately, it was not the safest place in the world for me. But I will tell you about that in a little while.

Everyone was in a much better mood. They even started to laugh about all the things that happened on the picnic. You would think that after a picnic like this one, they would never want to go on another picnic again. You would think they had learned their lesson. But the Duffs are not like that.

"Isn't nature wonderful?" sighed Mrs. Duff.

"It sure is," said Mr. Duff. "If you survive."

That's Mr. Duff's idea of a joke.

"Let's go on another picnic next week-end!" said Mrs. Duff.

"Great," said Beth. "Maybe I can find those baby snakes."

"This time," said Arnie, "I'll be in charge of bringing the matches and building the fire."

I felt my teeth starting to grind.

"That would be neat," said Mike. "I think all the pictures I got today were ruined by the rain."

"Good," said Katie. "They were dumb pictures."

Too bad about the pictures, I thought. There were some totally awesome rescues in there. Just because Katie didn't look like Miss America was beside the point. She never liked pictures of herself anyway—for some silly reason. It probably had to do with her hairdo. Maybe she would look better during rescues if she did something about her split ends.

I felt a bit depressed. I was thinking of the

picture Mike took of me towing the boat full of Duffs into shore. But then I cheered up. After all, I could always trust the Duffs to give me another chance at a daring rescue. Something just as good would probably happen next weekend.

Just then, Fudge came out on the porch. He was carrying a piece of newspaper in his mouth. He raced right over to me. I was feeling peaceful and happy. But then Fudge showed me the piece of newspaper.

"I cut this out for you, Mom," he said.

I took a look.

Aaaarrrrgh!

It was a picture of a kitten and a dog kissing!

"Isn't that a great picture?" said Fudge. "It's just like you and me!"

"It is not!" I said.

I closed my eyes. I always close my eyes when Fudge is bothering me. Normally, when I do this, Fudge thinks I'm asleep. Then he goes away. But Fudge did not go away.

"I'm going to make a whole collection of pictures just like this one," said Fudge.

"Don't bother," I said. "Those are stupid pictures."

"Oh, good," said Fudge. "You really aren't asleep! I always thought you were asleep when your eyes were shut."

I realized I had just made a terrible mistake. Now I will never be able to get Fudge to leave me alone.

"You know what I'm going to do with the pictures?" asked Fudge.

"No," I said. "And I don't want to know, either."

"I'm going to take the whole collection down to the newspaper office," he said.

"What for?" I said.

"I want the newspaper to have a special article just about the love that cats and dogs have for each other."

I decided not to say a word.

"Maybe Mike can get a picture of you and me kissing," said Fudge. "I want that picture right on the front page—bigger than the rest!"

No way, I thought. And to think I was upset about another picnic! This kissing-cat-and-dog-picture problem was the worst problem I had ever faced. My honor was at stake! My image was about to be ruined. My reputation would be in the toilet!

I vowed right then and there never to close my eyes around that awful Fudge again—especially if Mike and his camera were in the room.

Why me? I thought. What next?

I hated to even think about it.

THE END